Beverly Billingsly Borrows a Book

by Alexander Stadler

SILVER WHISTLE

HARCOURT, INC.

San Diego   New York   London

Requests for permission to make copies of any part of the work
should be mailed to the following address:
Permissions Department, Harcourt, Inc.,
6277 Sea Harbor Drive, Orlando, Florida 32887-6777.

www.harcourt.com

Silver Whistle is a trademark of Harcourt, Inc.,
registered in the United States of America and/or other
jurisdictions.

Library of Congress Publication-in-Data
Beverly Billingsly borrows a book/Alexander Stadler.
p. cm.
"Silver Whistle."
Summary: Beverly is thrilled to finally check out a book with her
own library card, but when she accidentally keeps the book too long
she worries that she'll have to pay a huge fine or go to jail.
[1. Books and reading—Fiction. 2. Libraries—Fiction.
3. Librarians—Fiction. 4. Worry—Fiction.] I. Title.
PZ7.S77573Be 2002
[E]—dc21   2001001548
ISBN 0-15-202510-3

H G F E

Printed in Singapore

To my mother and father, for brains;
to Janet E. Mather, for courage;
and to Andy, for a heart

—A. S.

Every Tuesday afternoon, Beverly Billingsly went to the library with her mother. Beverly loved the library. And this Tuesday would be even more special than usual.

"Is today the day I get my own card?" Beverly asked.

"Yes," answered her mother.

Mrs. Del Rubio was the new librarian.

Beverly straightened her bow and said, "I would like a library card, please."

"Wonderful," said Mrs. Del Rubio, as she finished shelving some books. "Please follow me to my desk."

Mrs. Del Rubio had a long list of questions. Beverly answered each one correctly. Her mother didn't have to help her with a single thing.

A few seconds later, Mrs. Del Rubio looked Beverly straight in the eye and said, "Miss Billingsly, you are now a member of the Piedmont Public Library. You may take out any book you like."

Beverly searched the shelves until she found what she wanted—
a big shiny book called *Dinosaurs of the Cretaceous Period*.

As Mrs. Del Rubio stamped the book, she said, "Remember to return it by April seventh."

iguanodon

Ankylosorus

Beverly loved *Dinosaurs of the Cretaceous Period*. She couldn't put it down. On Wednesday, after school, she studied the iguanodon. On Thursday and Friday, she read about the ankylosaurus.

She spent several days building a prehistoric jungle habitat.

Beverly read everywhere—at the dinner table, in bed, even in the tub.

On Monday morning, Beverly woke up early to finish the final chapter, "Eating Habits of the Triceratops."

As she turned the last page, she saw, stamped inside the back cover: RETURN BY APRIL 7.

Beverly looked at her calendar. The date was April eighth.

"Oh no," she whispered. "I'll return it today after school," she told herself.

At lunch, Beverly sat next to Sheila Rose Hoffstetter. "Do you know what happens when a person is late returning a library book?" Beverly asked.

"I'm not sure," Sheila said, "but I think you have to pay a lot of money."

"Like how much?" asked Beverly.

"Oh, like a thousand dollars, I think," answered Sheila.

Carlton Chlomsky had been listening to their conversation.
"My mother's friend's cousin's brother was late with a library book,
and he went to jail," Carlton said.

"I can't believe it!" said Beverly.

"Believe it," said Carlton, munching on a carrot.

That afternoon, as she was walking toward the library, Beverly's stomach started to ache. "Maybe I'll return the book tomorrow," she said to herself in a small voice.

Beverly didn't eat much at dinner. "I'm not hungry," she told her parents.

"Even with chocolate cake for dessert?" asked her mother.

"Is anything wrong?" asked her father.

Beverly shook her head and went to bed.

That night, Beverly had a strange and frightening dream. A big green triceratops stuck its head through her window.

"Return meeeee!" it growled. "Return me, Beverleeeeeee! I am overduuuuuuuuuuue! Return me or I will gobble you up!"

"But you're an herbivore!" Beverly shouted. "You eat only small plants and other vegetation! It says so on pages forty-two and forty-three!"

Suddenly Beverly woke up. Her mother was sitting on the edge of her bed.

"What's the matter, Beverly?" her mother asked.

"I have to return the book, and the dinosaur is mad at me, and Mrs. Del Rubio is going to take all my money, and I don't want to go to jail!"

Mrs. Billingsly smoothed the fur on Beverly's ears and gave her shoulder a little squeeze.

"Don't worry, honey," she said. "Nobody ever went to jail for an overdue library book. Tomorrow we'll go and return the book together."

The next day, after school, Beverly and her mother went to the library.

Beverly took a deep breath as she walked up to Mrs. Del Rubio's desk. "My book is overdue," she said.

Mrs. Del Rubio opened the book to the back. "Well, it's only a couple of days late, dear," she said. "We won't worry about it. Just try to be more careful next time." And then she closed the book and smiled.

"Now isn't that funny?" said Mrs. Del Rubio. "Oliver Shumacher walked in here not five minutes ago and asked about this very book. I think he's in your grade. Shall we take it to him?"

"Hi," said Oliver.

"Hello," said Beverly. "What are you working on?"

"I'm doing a report on pterodactyls," said Oliver.

"Did you know there was one that had a fifty-foot wingspan?" asked Beverly.

"And it could still fly?!" asked Oliver.

"Yes," said Beverly. "Here, I'll show you. There's a picture of one in chapter eleven."

And that is how the Piedmont Dinosaur Club began.

The illustrations in this book were done in gouache
and ink on Bristol Board.
The display type was set in Caslon Antique.
The text type was set in Utopia.
Color separations by Bright Arts Ltd., Hong Kong
Printed and bound by Tien Wah Press, Singapore
Production supervision by Sandra Grebenar and Wendi Taylor
Designed by Ivan Holmes